Yasmin and Dad went to the

1

Next, they went shopping.

Yasmin held the shopping list.

belt
golf ball
lamp

Yasmin and Dad went to a big shop. They got in the lift.

A man got in with them.

8

Yasmin and Dad got back in the lift.

The man got in with them.

Yasmin and Dad went back home.